Please return/renew this item by the last date
shown. Books may be renewed by
telephoning, writing to or calling in at any
library or on the Internet.

Northamptonshire Libraries and Information Service

Northamptonshire
County Council

www.northamptonshire.gov.uk/leisure/libraries/

For **Sarah, my wonderful**
Ricky Rocket illustrator

 Find out more about **Ricky Rocket** at
www.shoo-rayner.co.uk

First published in 2006 by Orchard Books
First paperback publication in 2007

ORCHARD BOOKS
338 Euston Road, London NW1 3BH
Orchard Books Australia
Hachette Children's Books
Level 17/207 Kent St, Sydney, NSW 2000

ISBN-13: 978 1 84616 395 1 (paperback)

Text and illustrations © Shoo Rayner 2006

3 5 7 9 10 8 6 4 (paperback)

Printed in Great Britain

Orchard Books is a division of Hachette Children's Books.

Rebel Flyer

Shoo Rayner

ORCHARD BOOKS

"MUM! Ricky's left his PE kit
at school!"

Ricky Rocket, the only Earth
boy on the planet of Hammerhead,
gritted his teeth.

Ricky's little sister, Sue, was the only Earth girl on the planet of Hammerhead, and the most irritating Earth girl in the *universe*. She loved getting him into trouble.

"Just wait till I get you!"
Ricky snarled.

"Mum!" Sue squealed. "Ricky says he's going to get me!"

"Didn't!"

"Did!"

"Didn't!"

"Did!"

Ricky grabbed Sue's pigtails and pulled them hard.

Sue went rigid. Her eyes lit up with a strange, powerful force. She opened her mouth as wide as a Hammerhead Cave Shark.

The air filled with the ear-splitting, blood-curdling, brain-jamming scream that little Earth girls are famous for all over the universe.

"ENOUGH!" Mum yelled. "Ricky – did you leave your PE kit at school? You know I need to get it cleaned."

Ricky stared at his shoes and nodded. Sue looked triumphant.

"You'll forget your head one day," Mum sighed. "Go and tidy your rooms, both of you, and stop fighting!"

HAMMERHEAD
CAVE SHARKS

Think twice before you swim in the cool, pink seas of Hammerhead. **Danger** lurks beneath the surface in the shape of **Cave Sharks!**

Cave Sharks are unique. They can open their jaws **180°** wide, revealing a hundred **pin-sharp** teeth. They will eat **anything!**

Actual Size

Luckily, **Cave Sharks** are only 8 mm long.

The next day, Sue was even more irritating.

"I'm bored!" she announced every five minutes.

"Ask a friend round to play," Mum suggested.

"She hasn't got any friends," Ricky laughed. "Poor, lonesome Sue."

Sue flew at Ricky and they tussled like Godzillian pythons.

Ricky's communicator *breeped*
in his room. He raced upstairs
to answer it.

"Mum?" Ricky shouted down
the staircase. "Can I meet Bubbles
in the park?"

"All right," Mum shouted back, "but you'll have to take Sue with you."

"No way!" Ricky retorted.

"You can both come shopping instead, if you like," Mum smiled up at him. "I need a new outfit for Aunt Milly's wedding on Earth next month."

"Urgh!" said Ricky. "OK, OK, I'll take her, but she'd better not be a pain or else…"

WHAT TO DO INSTEAD OF SHOPPING WITH MUM

Anything is better than shopping with Mum.

1 Clean out the Thingy Pig cage.

2 Have a shower every day for a week.

3 Get eaten by **three million** Cave Sharks.

4 Do homework.

X+Y= 42

5 Be kind to little sisters.

"Sit still!" Ricky grunted, forcing Sue into the passenger seat of his rocket and pulling the straps as tight as they would go.

"Hey!" Sue complained. "I can hardly breathe!"

"Good!" Ricky pointed a finger. "Don't move a quantum blip. I don't want to hear a squeak out of you. I'm the captain of this ship and you have to obey my orders."

Ricky shut the door tight and checked that his trusty rocket was ready for take-off.

The engine shuddered as Ricky pulled back the controls, guiding the rocket into the air.

"Course 321," he told the computer.

"Estimated time of journey: three minutes," it replied.

Hammerhead Park is the place to go for fun, fun, fun!

Park your flyer and feed the **Grucks** by the pond.

You can buy **Super Nova**[SR] and **Fizzywizzy**[SR] at the café.

Test your **flying skills** on the flyer course.

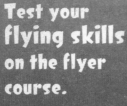

THE CANYONS

(Remember: fly safe!)

HAMMERHEAD PARK

Strap yourself into a swing and get hurled round in all directions. Shout "Giddy up!" when you've had enough.

Adjust the level of the gravity slides to go fast or slow, or to slide back up again.

Hold on tight!

The Twirtle will make you sick faster than a soft-boiled Dreg.

Bubbles watched as Ricky's rocket
touched down in the park.

He nodded at Sue. "Did you
have to bring *her*?"

22

"Yeah, sorry," Ricky apologised.
"We'll just have to see how good
a passenger she is!"

"What do you mean?" Sue
sounded suspicious.

Bubbles giggled. "Never been on the Flyer Course before, have you?"

"Let's start in the Canyons!" Ricky said. "Then we'll hit the Spin Tube. Sue will *love* that!"

HAMMERHEAD
PARK

FLYER COURSE BASICS

The flyer course is the main attraction at Hammerhead Park.

THE CANYONS

Weave your way through the Canyons - don't crash into the walls!

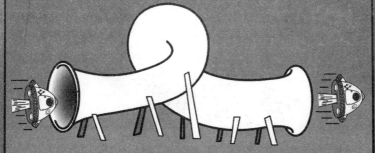

Zip into the Spin Tube and feel the G-forces as you are spun around 360°.

For advanced flyers only - must have proficiency level 2.

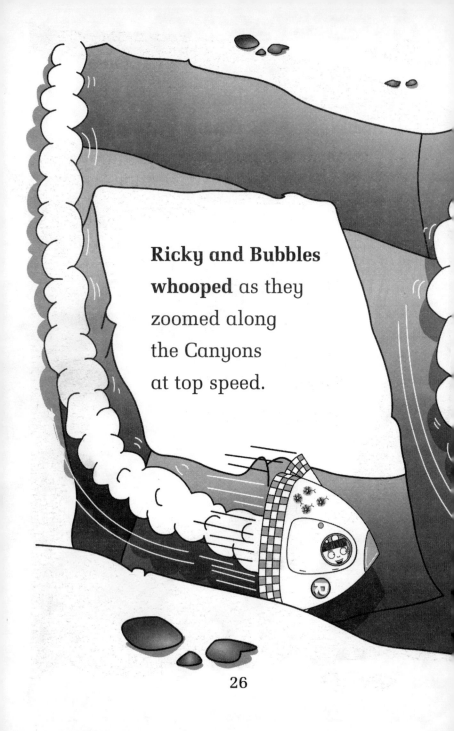

Ricky and Bubbles whooped as they zoomed along the Canyons at top speed.

Sue's panicked voice filled their headsets. "Ricky! Don't go so fast! Ricky! Look out! Ricky! I think I'm going to be sick!"

"Keep your helmet on, Sue!"
Ricky yelled. "We're going into
the Spin Tube!"

Sue screamed. "Ricky! There's another flyer right above us!"

Ricky looked up. "What on Hammerhead...?"

A sleek, dark shape barged into Ricky's airspace. From the corner of his eye, Ricky saw the badge of the Evil Lord Vorg. It was a new Rebel Flyer 250 – those machines were fast!

The Rebel powered ahead of
him into the Spin Tube. Still
flying at top speed, they were
hurled into a giddying spin.

Sue was screaming in Ricky's headset. He didn't know if he was up or down or about to crash into the crazy Rebel in front of him.

Suddenly they were out and in daylight again. The Rebel turned in a tight circle and came straight back at him.

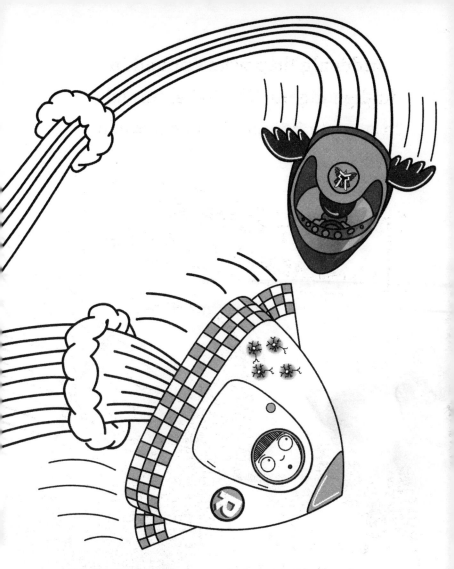

Ricky's rocket engines screamed
as he forced his trusty craft away
from certain disaster!

Ricky landed by the swings and
Bubbles touched down next to him.

"Did you see that?" Ricky said.
"Who does he think he is?"

"We're about to find out,"
said Bubbles.

The rebel craft touched down and
the canopy slid open. The pilot was big.
Slowly, he removed his dark helmet.
It was Grip, the biggest, meanest boy
in Ricky's class.

"Got ya little sister to fly for you,
eh, Ricky?" Grip taunted. "Or was
that you, flying like a little girly?"

No one called Ricky a little girly and got away with it. "Stay inside!" he hissed at Sue. "I'll handle this."

Grip stepped out of the Rebel Flyer. He towered over Ricky. His sharp, yellow teeth gleamed.

"They shouldn't let you fly that thing," Ricky said defiantly. "You're really dangerous."

"Oooh! Listen to the little girly. Isn't he tough?" Grip pushed Ricky – just enough to make him stumble.

"Hey!" Bubbles said, rushing to Ricky's side.

A ball of energy elbowed past
Ricky and Bubbles.

"Sue!" Ricky called. "I told
you to stay in the rocket!"

It was too late. Sue planted herself
firmly in front of Grip. "You leave my
brother alone, you bully!" she spat.

Grip laughed. "Ha! Ricky Rocket has
to get his little girly sister to fight for
him, too!"

Sue went rigid. A strange, powerful force lit up her eyes. *"Don't – call – me – a – little – girly!"* she growled.

"Oh dear," Ricky smiled at Grip. "You've done it now!"

Sue threw her head back and opened her mouth even wider than a Hammerhead Cave Shark.

The air filled with that ear-splitting,
blood-curdling, brain-jamming scream
that little Earth girls are famous for
all over the universe.

Grip's eyes popped, his teeth jangled in their sockets and his brain fried in his head. He opened his mouth and tried to speak, but no sound came out.

When he could move again, he ran
back to the Rebel Flyer

and screeched off
without another word.

"Yeah!" Ricky punched the air. "Fly away home, Grippy Wippy! Run back to your mummy."

Bubbles was amazed. A stream of bubbles poured from his trumpets. "W—w—ell done, Earth girl!" he stammered.

Sue smiled sweetly. "I think I'd like to play on the swings now," she announced.

"After that performance," Ricky laughed, "you can do anything you like!"

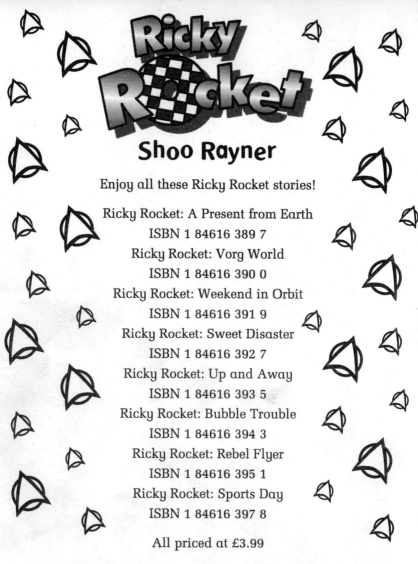

Ricky Rocket

Shoo Rayner

Enjoy all these Ricky Rocket stories!

All priced at £3.99

Orchard Crunchies are available from all good bookshops, or can be ordered
direct from the publisher: Orchard Books, PO BOX 29, Douglas IM99 1BQ
Credit card orders please telephone 01624 836000 or fax 01624 837033
or visit our internet site: www.wattspub.co.uk or e-mail: bookshop@enterprise.net for details.

To order please quote title, author and ISBN and your full name and address.
Cheques and postal orders should be made payable to 'Bookpost plc.'
Postage and packing is FREE within the UK
(overseas customers should add £1.00 per book).

Prices and availability are subject to change.